The Hare
and
The Tortoise

CAROL JONES

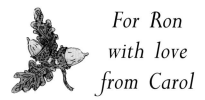

For Ron
with love
from Carol

Copyright © Carol Jones 1996

First American edition 1996
Originally published in Australia by HarperCollins*Publishers* Pty
Limited as an Angus & Robertson book

Walter Lorraine 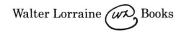 Books

For information about this and other Houghton Mifflin trade
and reference books and multimedia products, visit The Bookstore
at Houghton Mifflin on the World Wide Web at:
http://www.hmco.com/trade/.

Library of Congress Cataloging-in-Publication Data

Jones, Carol.
    The hare and the tortoise / [retold by] Carol Jones.
            p.   cm.
    Summary: Sure of winning the race with a tortoise, a hare dawdles
    about to make it more fun.
    ISBN 0-395-81368-9
    1. Toy and movable books--Specimens. [1. Fables. 2. Toy and
    movable books.] I. Aesop. II. Hare and the tortoise. III. Title.
PZ8.2.J655Har   1996
398.24'52792--dc20
[E]
                                        96-6439
                                          CIP
                                          AC

Printed in Hong Kong
10 9 8 7 6 5 4 3 2 1

The Hare
and
The Tortoise

CAROL JONES

Houghton Mifflin Company
Boston 1996

The air was clear and crisp as a new day dawned in the forest.
Down a winding trail jogged Hare on his regular early morning
training run. Out from a hole in the ground popped the sleepy
head of Mole. He had been awakened by the thumping on his bedroom ceiling.

'Inconsiderate fellow!' Mole grumbled, as Hare disappeared
around a bend in the track.
'He wakes me every morning
on his training run.'

Hare, with his chest
puffed out as he jogged,
called out loudly to
no-one in particular,
'I'm the fastest runner
in the forest. No-one can
beat me!'

That same morning Tortoise was enjoying a bowl of lettuce and dandelion soup for breakfast while catching up on the news in the *Forest Daily*. As usual, Hare was featured in the sports section. He had won yet another important race and the report suggested that Hare may become the forest's first Olympic champion.

Tortoise frowned.
'Hare really is becoming
a little too confident
for his own good.'

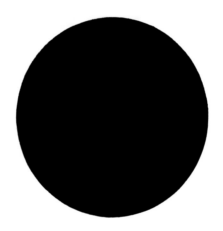

Y ou lazy Tortoise sitting down all day,' said Hare scornfully. 'You'll never stay fit and healthy fishing!'

It beats running around in circles. What's that good for?' replied Tortoise casting his line out into the river.

Everyone knows that I'm the fastest hare in the forest and that I win every race I'm in,' boasted Hare.

It's not always the fastest who wins,' muttered Tortoise. 'Especially when he is so silly and boastful.'

Silly am I?' retorted Hare frowning indignantly. 'And boastful? I'll show you a thing or two. Let's settle this with a race?'

Excellent!' agreed Tortoise. 'A race of about ten miles would suit me fine,' he said smiling confidently to himself.

H are couldn't believe his ears. He threw back his head and laughed until the tears ran down his furry face. 'You're the foolish one!' he chortled. 'You know I'm the champion of the forest and that no-one can beat me.'

'We'll see,' replied Tortoise. 'I'll race you next Saturday at noon.'

'You're on,' sniggered Hare. 'Ten miles next Saturday. See you then.'

Hare raced off quickly, eager to begin some more training.

Meanwhile Tortoise had finished his breakfast and reading the paper. He looked out the window and saw that it was a fine, sunny morning. 'Just the perfect day for a spot of fishing,' he thought. 'I'll try and catch some fish for lunch.'

Tortoise packed his fishing basket, slung it over his back and ambled off towards the stream. A friendly Willy Wagtail offered Tortoise a worm for bait and a snail decided to tag along for the ride.

Tortoise had just settled down happily by the stream with his fishing rod, when Hare came racing by. Hare stopped, did some stretching exercises and eyed Tortoise with disdain.

Farther down the track Hare stopped near a sturdy oak tree. Mrs Squirrel was farewelling her children as they left for school. Hare loved an audience. He reached up to an overhanging branch and began doing chin-ups.

Badger came out of his front door to collect his milk and paper. He frowned and gave Hare a disapproving look.

'Seventeen, eighteen, nineteen, twenty,' panted Hare.

'What a conceited show-off,' muttered Badger to Mrs Squirrel.

Hare raced on, past the halfway mark. On a long straight stretch of the course he looked back but Tortoise was nowhere in sight.

'What a stupid race,' Hare remarked to a group of spectators lining the course. 'I should never have agreed to such a ridiculous challenge. It's really beneath my dignity.'

As he was so far in front, Hare decided to have a rest. He sat down beneath a shady tree and pulled off his new running shoes. He closed his eyes and the sweet aromas of the forest flowers wafted past his nose and soon lulled him off into a deep sleep. His body was very tired from all the hard training he'd been doing every morning and evening.

The sun was going down when the determined figure of Tortoise shuffled past. A smile appeared on his face when he glanced at the sleeping hare.

Tortoise's supporters were delighted to see Hare sound asleep. 'We hope you sleep all night,' they chuckled.

Now that he was in the lead, a happy Tortoise plodded on enjoying the encouragement of his forest friends.

A family of frogs jumped into their pond and splashed water all over Tortoise to cool him down. He was feeling very hot under his shell after so many hours of trudging along the race track.

'Thank you so much, frogs. I appreciate your help and encouragement,' he said politely.

At the same time Tortoise had just managed to drag his back feet across the starting line. Hedgehog, feeling sorry for his friend, decided he would accompany Tortoise to give him some support.

A stern Badger called out to Hedgehog. 'If you assist Tortoise in any way he will be disqualified.'

Tortoise smiled to himself. He was happy to plod along at his own pace knowing he had the support of his friends.

Hare raced away from the start like an express train. He was soon around the first bend in the race and setting a cracking pace which caused some rabbits, who were sauntering across the track, to jump out of the speedster's way.

'Poor old Tortoise doesn't have a chance,' said one of the young rabbits.

In no time at all, Hare passed the fence where Owl, one of the course officials, was sitting.

'Give my regards to Tortoise when you see him in an hour or two,' Hare sniggered as he raced off towards the halfway mark.

AT
12 Noon
A Race
between
HARE
&
TORTOISE

Hare arrived early for the race, sporting a brand new pair of air-cushioned running shoes. Immediately on arrival he began doing an elaborate series of stretching and warm-up exercises.

Finally, with only two minutes to the starting time, Tortoise ambled up to the starting line.

'I was just about to claim a forfeit,' said Hare, 'and then I could have a decent race with my friends.'

Tortoise ignored Hare's taunts. A very serious Badger gave the pair the race instructions. 'We'll have no jostling at the start and no cutting off,' he said. 'Now take your marks.'

Before he crouched down Hare sneered at Tortoise. 'I'll wait for you at the finishing line — but only for one hour!'

Tortoise didn't reply but just smiled to himself. Badger dropped a red handkerchief to start the race and, amid some excited cheering from the spectators, they were off.

It was the day of the race. Everyone in the forest was excited about the challenge and wanted to be part of it.

Badger had appointed himself as the race referee and had nailed up the race rules. A group of young rabbits under Mr Fox's supervision were sent out to mark the course with red flags.

Mole popped his head out to see what all the activity was about. When he learned of the race, Mole became an immediate supporter of Tortoise.
'That young upstart of a hare needs to be taken down a peg or two.'

But Hare was not without his own support.
A group of hares from his running club had turned up, ready to have a good laugh at Tortoise's expense.

It was nearly evening when Hare awoke with a start.
An ant had bitten him on the leg. Hare rubbed his eyes
and stared in disbelief. Tortoise was way ahead and near the finishing line!
A feeling of panic gripped Hare. He grabbed his shoes and raced off, not
even stopping to put them on. He ran faster than he'd ever run before.

'I must win,' he panted. 'My reputation depends on it.
I'll never live it down if a
tortoise beats me.'

Owl and Mole stared in
disbelief as Hare
flashed by.

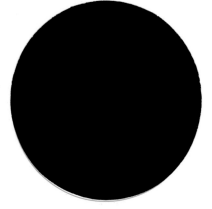

Tortoise was given a rousing welcome as he plodded towards the finishing line.

'Tortoise is going to win!' shouted a surprised little rabbit.

'Maybe not,' replied his friend. 'Look! Here comes Hare!' Down the track flew Hare, travelling so fast that his legs didn't appear to be touching the ground.

Tortoise ambled on.

Hare made a desperate lunge at the finishing line, but it was too late. Tortoise had just pulled himself across.

'You've beaten me!' gasped an infuriated Hare.

Tortoise turned slowly towards his rival. 'Yes,' he said with a smile. 'You teased me because I was not as fast as you, but ...

Slow and Steady Wins the Race